STILL WATERS RUN DEEP

STILL WATERS RUN DEEP

Aliya Cooper

Aliya Cooper
2016

First Printing: 2016

ISBN: 978-1-365-22025-8

To all the dreamers

GENESIS

Running through 4-lane traffic, cold and wet, dropping to my knees and wishing for death in the form of an 18-wheeler. Yearning for that eternal, nameless peace that we wish upon the dead but never the living. She cowered, crouching beneath the overpass. The rain fell around her, and the traffic sped by. No one could see her in the darkness. She felt lost, alone, and she longed to be found. If she remained lost, perhaps she would disappear, fade away into the background, into the darkness, into the sound of rain on asphalt. She was cold and shaking. Life was as dismal as this stormy night. She had lost all ability to cope. The autumnal leaves lay wet and dirty on the roadside. Then with more courage than she had possessed in her lifetime, she darted into traffic, in front of a large truck that had no chance of stopping in time. She ran into inevitability. She ran into her destiny. She ran into death and all the mystery therein. She ran into eternal peace.

I didn't die that day, but as far as you know I could be penning this account from beyond the grave. In heaven or the underworld or a million places between. Something happened that day, a searing. I can hear the hiss of heated contact as I form a memory of the events that followed, and they were forever burned into my mind. My life took a different route from the one I expected. For the better, I think. I don't know. Who can know that? Just the insurmountable forces of fate. I know now that things are starting to make sense.

So, how do I begin? Where does one put their foot when they begin the journey of a life? The womb, the first memory, or perhaps at the first fork in the road (when they first knew that their lives were going to be a bit different)? However, considering this is my story, and I, for once, have control, I will begin where I damn well please.

The sky is a strange shade of smoky auburn, and I feel it is foreboding. I find it difficult to imagine a grand life outside the small unremarkable one which I now lead. The oncoming headlights seem ethereal, predestined. There might have been rain. Or sun. Even snow or perhaps fire and brimstone would have escaped my minimum security memory. What I recall is the tempest that raged within (me).

SPAIN

It was a dream I've had for a while, made of distant subconscious memories of travel shows and magazine photos and a few semesters of high school Spanish.

It was summer in the Plaza del Sol. The area was full of tourists, and the Spanish sun burned bright and high in the sky.

Her whole life she dreamt of the Spanish Mediterranean, of crossing the ocean and erasing memories, unmaking the past, a kind of trans-Atlantic amnesia. Everything that happened in this life would be as if it had happened to someone else. But every year that passed and this dream became a little more impossible, it began to seem cruel. This empty promise of reinvention, of redemption, began to haunt her, doomed to become another distant shore she would never reach. Hope crunched up in one hand from ferocious desire. She would walk into the sea and drown a metaphorical death or—in her dreams at least—sail to distant shores where all that is lost can be found.

My memories of that place are at times more vivid than those of reality.

THE MACHINERY OF NIGHT

It was one of those dark cold New York nights they write songs about. A girl, fidgeting and shaking slightly, was in an alley, an older man standing beside her, his hands in the pockets of his leather jacket.

"You got cash?"

"Yeah. How much?" She was impatient.

"I can give it to you for 80."

"Eighty. What the fuck, man? All I have is 40."

"You're shit out of luck then." He began to walk away.

"Come on, man." She had desperation in her eyes, and he smiled.

"How about we work out a trade?" He grinned.

She walked inside the abandoned warehouse, and all she remembered after that was flying or it felt like she was flying. It always did after she got high. The sound of the needle clattering to the floor, the man laughing and zipping up his pants, her panties in a ball in her fist, all that was gone. She wasn't half-naked lying on some cold floor littered with needles and piss, 12 degrees outside. She was in the clouds, and all the shit that was weighing down on her was gone, lifted, and she leaned her back against the wall and closed her eyes. She sighed.

She woke up in a cold sweat in her bed. Immediately she knew the day to come would be long as hell. Instinctually she touched her arms where the tracks left behind by years of self-destruction were still quite visible. With her scars still so tangible, she could never forget. That part of her life wasn't going to disappear anytime soon. Even here, it didn't really matter where she ran, it would always be right there behind her eyelids waiting to reach out like a skeleton and pull her back into a drug haze of heroin and rough sex with nameless strangers. She went to the bathroom and threw up. She lay on the bathroom rug, breathing heavily, eyes closed, waiting for the yearning to pass. A part of her would always want to take flight. But that part of her had to be grounded, chained, have its wings clipped. She would be a junkie for the rest of her life, but she'd rather be a recovering one. One with her dignity and her life.

She got up off the floor and turned on the shower before sitting on the toilet, her head in her hands. She didn't have to get up for work for another couple of hours but there'd be no sleeping after this. So she just thought she might as well get up. She took off the oversized T-shirt she slept in and looked in the mirror for a moment. She wasn't fat but she wasn't skinny either. In her mind, she had fat gathering in all the wrong places and her shoulders were too big for a woman. She had never felt beautiful but guessed that most other women probably hadn't either. She didn't let it bother her too much. She was never one for vanity. She stepped under the hot water and let it run over her face and then down her back, heating wherever it ran. She sighed and put her hands against the wall. The voice in the back of her mind whispered to her, What are you doing?

"I don't know," she muttered.

Her life seemed split in two. There was the part that came before, the drugs, the bruises, even back to when she was just a shy girl without many friends who worked a job in a movie theater she hated. And then there was the part that came after of which she was writing the current chapter here, trying to forget that her book ever had a prequel.

She worked 10 hours a day 6 days a week at a bar that she hated. This was her life and she was trying her best to accept it, to make the most of it. It was the end of the night, and she was wiping down the tables outside. For a moment, she just stood and closed her eyes, letting the summer breeze play in her hair. It was quiet there, and for that she was grateful. She paused, and sighed, with the rag in her hand until her boss called out to her. She snapped back into reality and finished her work, even sweeping up the toilet paper that littered the bathroom floor.

MY OWN PRIVATE INFERNO: I ♥ NY

"Nel mezzo del camin' di nostra vita, mi ritrovai per una selva oscura." In the middle of our life's road, I found myself in a dark wood. Dante understood that escape was impossible.

That's how I ended up here in a kind of perdition. I lost my way, and before my era of madness consumed me wholly, I knew I had to flee or forever be condemned. That's when I decided to run away from my life. I set out on a journey of forgetfulness, of throwing myself into a dense black hole where hopefully I would be utterly destroyed or at least come out on the other side with no memories and and no past.

I was lost but I came here to lose myself. And let me tell you there's no better place. This huge, tiny island, shared by junkies and billionaires alike. Crackhouses and Versaces. Granted, not on the same block but separated only by an invisible line that all see but few dare cross. You can see the exact shade of green of that other grass but that shimmering, dividing line may as well be a DMZ riddled with mines and barbed wire. We look at them across It but they do not deign to do the same except those rare souls who slip past the boundaries and find themselves in dark woods without even realizing it. The T-shirts say it best I suppose: I ♥ NY.

I had lost hope. Even for that, Dante said it best: "Lasciate ogni speranza voi ch'entrate." Abandon all hope, ye who enter here.

I WISH I KNEW WHY THE CAGED BIRD SINGS

I walked the streets. Alone. Night. I slipped into light and then darkness, passing under streetlights like heartbeats. The river flowed slowly to my right as it wound its way among willows and white-barked trees. If sunrise was my youth, then I am now in my darkest hour. An eclipse such as none had ever seen. A somber dawn without light. In ancient times, they believed that if you were forgotten, it was like you never existed. Your very soul disappeared from wherever it had taken up residence in the afterlife. At times I wanted to disappear, slip into oblivion, be erased. All the pain gone like a magic trick, an illusion. Now you see it, now you don't. I believed in second chances, just not two in the same life. I'm done. The only chance I'd ever get, I had destroyed with a needle and tears. I accepted my life now, such as it is. I was determined to never ask for more, to never wonder at my lot in my life, to never pursue happiness, because I didn't deserve it and because it would never come. I yielded to life as a caged bird.

"She was packed, she had a suitcase full of noble intentions. She had a map and straight face, hell-bent on reinvention. And she was ready for the lonely. She was in it for it only."

WARM DAYS, COLD NIGHTS

The utter silence stirred something in her as only silence could. The wind gently brushed the plants in the courtyard, but her mind was elsewhere. In closed bedrooms, in open plazas, in parks, restaurants, on the beaches of San Sebastian. Where her mind rested was warm and peaceful, but the reality against which dreams battle is a cruel, harsh, and hostile place. She lives there. She breathes it. She existed solely because it has not yet found reason to end her.

Mornings, though, were different. They were a gift. She felt guilty if she didn't take advantage. She took long walks through parks where she knew no one would bother her, look at her, wonder about her. She sat on the edge of fountains and closed her eyes, waiting for the world to fade away and the only sensation remaining that of the midday sun.

There was a kind of clarity that she had never known before. She saw the world for what it truly was and herself. In the past she was fighting against the current of life, unwilling to play the hand she was dealt. But now there was a calm within her. The calm borne of the end of struggle. No arguments, no fighting, no "what ifs." "What if" was a dangerous question and she knew it. Why wonder how things could have been when the past is absolute? She knew she could never change anything; she had spent her whole life hoping that things would suddenly change. But she had since given up childish pursuits.

With age and with time, we give up our ambitions. We release our hopes into the wind to be taken to faraway lands that we will never see. We let our dreams die the hard deaths we wish upon ourselves. Then life becomes a barren tundra full of an endless nothingness. A beautiful nothingness sans everything.

BECAUSE WE ARE ALSO WHAT WE HAVE LOST

There are so many moments I want back, that I'd do differently if I could. I mean, I'm sure everyone has them. I'm sure everyone wishes they could turn back the clock and right their mistakes, but I dwelled on it. I played back moments in my mind trying to find where I went wrong and driving myself insane with repetition before finally playing it as it should have gone, and that is the reality I accept. I punish myself, then I lie to myself. I have to if I want to survive. It's simple self-preservation.

I wear so many masks my life is a fucking masquerade ball. I play the parts that others want to see, but none of these people are me. I never let people see who I am beneath it all. I put up the walls of an impenetrable fortress and permit none to enter. I live in fear that they would come under the guise of friendship and lay siege, threatening flame and destruction. Or maybe upon looking upon the visage of the fair princess come to find that she is indeed the wicked and hideous stepmother and flee. But mostly I'm just passing the time until my time is up. That's what we're all doing, isn't it? Working our shitty jobs and suffering under the burden of our responsibilities, waiting. Waiting to be relieved, like Atlas, of the weight of the world.

HEARTS AND FLOWERS

I had never been in love. Never even had a boyfriend. I was a virgin for a long time. Until the drugs made me throw my inhibitions into the gutter. I don't remember losing my virginity. It wasn't one of those adolescent memories of fumbling in the bedroom of a suburban house vacant of parents or in the backseat of a car parked on a hill with some tawdry named like "Lover's Lane". I didn't know what I felt like to be desired or wanted. After a while, I grew used to be alone. I assumed I always would be. If my body had no worth, why not use it like life had used me? In my mind, I never had a path but maybe that's because I also believed I had no future. No promises, no destinations for me. But still miles to travel.

NIGHTMARES

Beneath the ground there lies the carcass of a young woman. The hollow soulless shell of a person unworthy of life. In a tomb, an unvisited sepulcher haphazardly placed on the side of a dusty unused road, there lay the remains of a young girl who was altogether unmemorable. Her name will not go down in books nor be spoken of past the days of her uneventful life. A hot lonely wind sweeps clouds of dust across the nameless gravestone. The sight is a desolate one, indeed, but the fate of being forgotten is unbearable. But I must imagine the young girl under the ground experiences now a kind of peace, regardless of the existence of heaven or hell. She rests in peace with the tombstone's only company: the midnight crows that circle constantly in their murder, waiting for the timely demise of some tragic carrion. She no longer suffers the pain of life. The girl beneath cruel earth is me.

I awoke in the twilight hours with the image of my death fresh on my brain. It's a strange lullaby indeed but it is the one that has haunted me and comforted me for as long as I can remember. Death is not a curse but a blessing. A blinding white light at the end of the darkest tunnel. It's good to know there's an end in sight. The thing we strive for, the dream yet to come to fruition. Death is my release from a lifetime of pain.

The moon is looming full and yellow outside my window. It looks like the moon of a fairy tale come down to earth, glowing like a celestial god, but I shake away foolish thoughts. There is a moment when I wake up every morning where, for a split second, I have forgotten everything and I'm blissfully happy. Then I remember everything all at once, (my job, paying bills, worrying about calling this person or that to ask some inane question to which they would reply in annoyance as if all humans knew whatever information I was ignorant of.) It all came rushing in like water to pull me down deeper with its heavy wet weight. I got out of bed simply out of fear of what would happen if I didn't. I thought I was being made to do something against my will all these years, but the truth was guiding my will, not the other way around.

REHAB

She woke to pain and blurred vision. She was unsure of where she was, and she was certain that sometime in the previous night, she had lost a fight with a sledgehammer. Slowly things began to come into focus. She was in a large building; other people slept scattered across the expansive floor. Old disused discarded furniture was haphazardly placed, and a harsh blue light streamed in through the dusty industrial windows. She put a hand to her head and she could feel the blood coursing through her head, could hear the rhythmic throbbing of rushing blood in her ears. She pushed herself onto her knees and got up slowly to her feet. She was dizzy and had to put a hand to the wall to walk. She found her way to the nearest open door. She was in a bathroom that hadn't been cleaned since the building was in operation. The stench of the various human fluids had been accumulating for some time and was almost too strong to bear but she was nauseous and didn't want to be sick outside. She stood in place for a while waiting for her will to move or leave or vomit to kick in. She walked a bit in front of a row of dirty sinks and broken mirrors above them. There were stalls lining the right wall, but she didn't want to chance touching the doors let alone going in one of them. As she looked to her left, she caught sight of the face of a stranger. She had a black eye and a bruise discolored her right cheek. There was blood under her nose that had been smeared across her face in a Van Gogh disaster. Her lip had been split and was swollen. She touched her face lightly and then closed her eyes. Then she leaned down and braced herself on the sink. She tried taking deep breaths, but she could already feel it rising up in her. She threw up. She didn't want to look at herself in the mirror again. And she didn't remember what happened to her.

"I can't do this," she whispered to herself. "I can't do this anymore." Tears streamed down her face and their salt stung her wounds.

* * *

I was standing outside the Pine Lake Rehabilitation Center with my hands in my pockets and my sunglasses on. I was looking up at the sign and wondering if I should even bother. I knew that in a few hours the shakes would start, and I imagined being in there and not being able to get out. I'm not good with confined spaces or cages, and this place seemed like a prison masquerading as a helping hand. I thought about getting high one last time before I went in. One last hit for the road.

Inside it was so clinical, the lines of chairs in the lobby, the security code you needed to get to the back rooms, the staff all dressed in white like in a sanitarium.

What the hell am I doing here?

I walked up to the front desk where the woman sat behind glass and she looked up at me with tired unpatient eyes. "Can I help you?"

"Umm....I'm checking in, I guess."

"All right, you'll need to fill out these forms and sign these papers where the X's are." She handed me a stack of papers, and I knew in that moment I would be signing away my life, my freedom, my past, and whoever I was before I walked into this lobby.

I sat down in the closest chair colored a kind of faded pink, and I stopped. I thought about everything that led up to this moment:

Then I just had to get out. I thought I might suffocate; I just got up and ran away. I found Frankie later that night and bought a stamp off him.

"Needle. Free with every purchase." It's what he always says.

I sat in the alley, one I'd slept in many a night, and I melted the shit on some foil. Funny I never smoked cigarettes or weed or anything before this. I couldn't work a lighter until 2 years ago. Now I'm a pro. Huh, a pro. The irony. Then I sucked it up into the syringe. I doubt Frankie got a fresh supply of needles in every week, I mean, it's not like he's a fucking hospital. So God knows where this needle has been. But I'm beyond giving a shit. I don't even bother looking for a vein. I just inject it fully into my arm. I use an old track to cut down on new marks but I'm just making the old ones look even worse. Whatever. I almost gave this up, I think to myself. I almost lost this feeling. Almost.

Waking up cold and hungry once again in an alley. A fire had been burning in a trash can all night and the scent of smoke and burned garbage was in the air. She rolled up from where she had been lying on the ground and start walking. It was morning, and the crisp sweet smell of a fresh day wafted through the air. She didn't know where but she just had to keep going forward. Walking through the streets of this city that she knew so well, she looked around for the first time in years. Calm marshmallow clouds float as lazily in the clear blue sky as the couples lying together on the grass. It seems like an eternity could pass me by in an instant. And it did. I see the old Jewish women on benches. Wrinkles run through faces like great canyons left by an ancient river. Great rifts left by the passage of time. All at once, age becomes a villain from which there is no escape. I walk the last few yards to where I squat, hidden beneath the cool shade of the little trees on this dreamy street. In a few short hours, the rose sky will fade to a plum tint, and a city that never sleeps takes a momentary repose from the hurried life it leads in the day (when the sun is ablaze). The first invisible stars will twinkle a lullaby I once knew by heart. With the twilight growing in my mind already descending upon this metropolis, I arrive back at the clinic afloat and adrift, filled with visions of the bluest sky.

* * *

They closed the door behind me and I heard the lock click into the place. It was the sound of finality. It took hours before the yearning started, that pull that usually whispered in my ear now was screaming, and I couldn't stop it. Soon I was screaming at the top of my lungs. "Get me the fuck out of here! You can't keep people locked up like this!" I found no rest that night, not in the bed where I beat my legs to distract from the screams nor the floor which was cold but could not assuage my hunger nor the wall where I beat my head hoping to empty it of everything, everything that came before, my past, who I was, what I had done, what I was feeling, all I would ever feel. All night I paced and screamed and cried and begged but I couldn't sleep. I threw up sporadically until there was nothing left inside. I was sweating but freezing at the same time. By morning I was hoarse and my eyes were bloodshot and I was still shaking. A nurse came in with water in a plastic cup and some hospital-quality food on a try and set it down next to me where I crouched in the corner.

"The first night's the hardest," she said quickly before leaving the room and clicking the lock once again.

Breakfast and then a daily ration of methadone followed by group. A bunch of addicts sitting around telling stories about all the horrible shit they did when they were high. Abandoning their babies, doing heroin while they were pregnant, robbing people, sharing needles. One guy had HIV, another had hepatitis. I didn't know what to say.

"Hey, umm, my name is June, and I've been on heroin for 3 years. I started using when I was 23 because…"

"Why?" the group psychiatrist asked.

"Because I didn't want to feel anything anymore." That was all I said. That was all I could say.

"Okay, next." he pointed to a woman sitting next to her with messy blonde hair and dark circles under her eyes.

"My name is Sarah. I was an addict for 5 years but I been clean for 2 months." She paused and looked down at the floor, gathering her courage to expose all her dirty laundry to a circle of people staring at her. "I done a lot of things I'm not proud of. The drugs, man, they make you someone else. Take you out of your head. I got two kids but Childrens' Services took 'em away when I was using. I gotta get clean so I can get 'em back."

I couldn't look at her. I just stared at the floor, too. Oh my god, I thought, she's me. They're all me. They're what I've become. We're ghosts, shadows of human beings. We're all damaged goods that maybe no one will ever want, that may never be useful again. I close my eyes and imagine myself as I was before. Timid, afraid, lonely, unsure. I always compared myself to others. I looked around and saw how much I was falling behind. In the movies, drugs make you numb. I wanted to be numb more than anything, damn the consequences.

"Darryl, would you like to go next?"

"Yeah. Umm, I'm Darryl. I been clean a month.

The shrink came up to me after group. "You know, you don't have to be afraid to share in group. No one will judge you. Everyone's been through a lot."

"Yeah, I know. I'm just not one to open up to strangers and 'share'. It's not me."

"Well, what can it hurt? Isn't it better to get it out than keep it locked away?"

I felt this becoming a bad talk show. "Sure, Doc. I'll be sure to spill my guts next time."

"That's not what I mean." He motioned to his open office door. "Come in."

"Sit down."

"I want you to be totally honest with me, but more importantly, honest with yourself. Why did you really start using?"

"Because it felt amazing, like it could go on forever. I didn't feel anything else, no self-loathing, no fear. I could look at myself in the mirror. If I could've, I would've been high all the time. Maybe it's not a bad way to live."

"It's a good way to die."

"I should've been so lucky."

"Are you suicidal?"

"What do you think?"

"Why do you want to die?"

"Why should I want to live? I've never understood what made living so fucking precious. I look into my future, and I don't see anything. What do I have to live for? There's nothing for me here. I wake up every morning and I feel sick, knowing that the day will be as empty and painful as the last."

"I think you need to change your perceptions."

"Don't feed me any of that mind over matter bullshit. This is my life and it will be until the day the die. So what am I waiting for? I'll never have the life I want. And giving up feels so good, it's easy. I need my life to be easy. For once."

"That's not realistic. No one's life is easy. No one's."

"Then what's the point. Suffering? Why?"

"It's called living."

"Well, I don't want it. I'm done with this life."

I walked out. I wanted to run out of the front door and find the nearest dealer who would help erase the past 3 weeks. But I stayed. I don't know why. If I was starting to buy into the bullshit or if some god or devil pushed me through the program, I don't know. But either way it happened. I was cured. Well, I should put that in quotations.

You should see my face now as I'm writing it. "I was cured." I'll never be cured, never be free of the proverbial monkey on my back. At least now the monkey is on a leash and only occasionally throws tantrums. But I started talking and I started getting to the heart of things. I still hated group but the one-on-one stuff wasn't so bad. I poured my heart out like a lovesick teenager. And I was surprised that he was still listening. No one really ever listened to me before. When I was younger, I used to talk really fast because I wanted to get out a complete thought before the listener totally lost interest in me and what I was saying.

My sessions were like exorcisms. It all just came out like a drunken confession.

"I wish I was more alive. I wish I lived in the moment. I wish I wasn't afraid all the time. I wish I didn't have to wish all the time. I wish…"

He listened quietly to what I was saying. I wasn't an open person, never showed my emotions, never let anyone in, so to spill my guts like this was uncharacteristic but I was feeling inexplicably liberated. After a lifetime of tortured silence, it was a change to have an open and non-judgmental ear. I let a stream of consciousness rush forth from me, letting its floodwaters carve canyons into my subconscious. I never believed in some psychological-based salvation but I had nothing to lose. I had for so long believed I was beyond salvation, that I was already dead but my body and mind refused to give up their toehold on life.

Later on, I would go and stand by the East River and watch the ebb and flow of its polluted waters and I felt as much adrift as those pieces of discarded plastic or the used condoms.

ANGEL-HEADED HIPSTERS

Drug den, crack house, how many names do you know for such a place? Where can you find them? And what place in the world is inhabited by those who frequent such places? Who are they? Why are they? Sometimes before the haze of chemical bliss overtook me, I would look around them and wonder who they were. Who was missing them? What happened to them so that we all ended up together imprisoned in hell? We all took different routes but they all led here to this dark, twisted wood worthy of Dante.

THE CITY

I think of this place differently now, this great city, this horrible city, the bridges that let us in but do not allow us to leave, of how we're all trapped together in this beautiful disaster. I look up now more than I ever have. It's amazing how you forget how blue the sky is or how the skyscrapers that seem so close to heaven leave us all in shadow and darkness.

She inhaled deeply and felt like she was breathing for the first time. Madrid (New York) smelled different, tasted different than it ever had before. This was her second chance, the one she didn't deserve but was going to take nonetheless.

As I watch the cars cast distorted reflections in the buildings' huge glass windows, I realized that this place is a kind of limbo, a place people get stuck when trying to reach worlds more real. How can any of these people feel happy or fulfilled living in a parallel universe, so much less real, so much less satisfying, less *here* than anywhere else in the world? I knew better than anyone how that felt.

"Aren't you afraid of dying?"

"It's not like I'm going to live forever. We all die someday. What does it matter if it's tomorrow or 40 years?"

"Most people think that time on earth is precious." My therapist, an old man with reading glasses.

"Good for them. I guess they have something to live for."

"And you don't?"

"Have you seen my life?"

"You can always change it."

"Yeah, right after I win the lottery and hell freezes over."

"Then why are you here?"

I paused for a second and looked down. "I don't know."

I don't know where in my timeline I stand, closer to the end or to the beginning. I don't know when my story ends. This could be my last chapter for all I know but at least I hope that whoever reads my story will think well of me and close the novel with a sense of hope or a sense that redemption is possible. Will I attain it is still left to be decided. (Or maybe just a sense of who I am because I sure as hell have no idea.)

"I wish people were honest with us from the beginning. I wish my parents had told me that I couldn't be anything I wanted to be when I was a little. I wish they had told me that certain doors were already closed to me, even before I was born. 'You'll never be president, or a model or an actress. You'll never be loved. You'll probably be alone for the rest of your life.' At least then we could prepare ourselves for it. Instead of clinging to hope like a life raft when we're all fucking drowning anyway. So then why all the lies?" The tears were streaming down my cheeks by this point. I had to turn away and gather myself. I covered my mouth with my hand and then wiped away the tears. Composure.

"Survival of the fittest, fucked if you are not."

*   *   *

Rehab was a parade of humiliation, but it saved my life. As I was leaving, the smiling staff patted me on the back and showered me with slogans.

"One day at a time."

"Don't be afraid to ask for help."

"Never be someone's slogan, because you are poetry." which I think they stole from a Sandra Bullock movie.

A few days later, I began work at an international conglomerate of large-scale supermarkets bordering on monopoly that will remain nameless. It was the kind of job retained by the truly desperate or the near-retired. No one who worked there was single. Everyone was either married, had children, or were so near the end of life, they approached every situation with a kind of calm. No use getting worked up over some silly mistake or pissed off customer of which there were many. It was the kind of place one could easily get lost, drifting along amidst the beeps of the scanners and swipes of the credit cards. I had a mini existential crisis daily, and it was a battle not to walk out on the spot. I left my old life for this? I thought. I had never been so blatantly aware of the dismal parade that could easily become my future. I imagined myself growing old there in front of a register, watching bananas, milk, and bread endlessly rolling down the conveyor belt to where they would be trapped in plastic bags, and I along with them, trapped in this monotonous hell. I had to get out. I worked there for what seemed an eternity before I had saved up enough to get myself across an ocean and the hell out of here. I didn't know what I was going to, but I knew what I was leaving: a soulless existence which would have killed my spirit long before my body.

STILL WATERS RUN DEEP

They say that still waters run deep which is to say that because the water isn't flowing, rushing, in constant motion, it can seep down into the earth farther than any white water rapids can go because it is unmoving, stationary, immobile. She knew she was those still waters. The surface looked calm, boring even, but beneath them was an entire mystery of life, just waiting to be discovered and explored, if anyone ever bothered. But no one ever did. She had never been desired, wanted. This was completely foreign to her. She had felt invisible for a large chunk of her life, always passed over for her friends who were inevitably beautiful. She was a good listener, the sidekick who was never once considered as dating material. She was a ghost among the living, a dandelion among roses, a duck among swans. She understood it was because she possessed none of the qualities the opposite sex seemed to be searching for in their partners, not beauty, not personality, not physical fitness. She was ill-shaped with shoulders that were too big and a round face, bad skin and more fat than she was ever comfortable with. She could not remember ever being comfortable in her own skin. It was difficult to accept, this life of loneliness that lay ahead, but the accepting wasn't the worst part. This was reserved for the loss of hope. It was nice at times to think that one's soul mate was just around the corner, but, I don't know, she felt it through and through, that there was no one waiting. No future of marriage, companionship, bliss. Her future was…empty. Utterly empty. Like there was a hole in the world, a bottomless pit of nothingness.

THE ART OF DYING

The pain came in waves. I had this vivid burst of consciousness: I am going to die. I have never believed in God and so, by extension, do not believe in hell. Never have. But I was afraid of death, afraid that something horrible waited beyond it.

The wound was on my right side and judging from the blinding pain, it went deep. I don't exactly remember what happened. When I felt the knife go in, the world stopped. I saw details of the alley I had never seen before. The lights of the passing cars were like beacons down a road I once traveled but have lately lost my way. I wanted to follow them, to see where the road ended and what lay there. I caught the scent of Chinese wafting from the restaurant next door, I heard cab drivers honking and the screeching of kamikaze wheels. I heard the laughter of passers-by, people who would go on and live their lives, grow old, share experiences that I would never have. I knew this was the end, something in my soul told me my time had run out. My descent seemed in slow motion as I fell on the cold, damp, smelly ground beneath a night sky completely devoid of stars. There was no white light, no choir of seraphim, not even a scythed figure in black come to claim me for a journey across the Styx. I just lay there, gasping, the blood staining my hands, my clothes, the earth beneath me. For a moment, everything became clear. I saw this whole other life. Life as it should have been. Then the world went blurry, and I closed my eyes. Come what may.

My next memory is of waking up. Nothing new, not the first time I woke up in a strange place, but this one was clinical, white and with the smell of death and vomit. I was dizzy and unable to focus. Doctors and nurses drifted in and out like alabaster ghosts, their voices slow and droning. I couldn't understand. I was deaf and dumb and utterly confused.

I woke up in the ER. There was an IV in my hand, and my right side was bandaged. I woke up here once before, after I'd OD'd. I don't recommend it. It felt like my veins were aflame, something like being burned alive from the inside out Spanish Inquisition-style. I was sure I was damned. I was sure I'd go to hell. Helplessness is not a comfortable sensation. It was a punishment having to give myself over to the pain. I watched the world grow smaller and smaller in my vision with sights and sounds becoming more and more distant. I was leaving this place, this body, going to the beyond to find out all the answers. To be damned, redeemed, deceived, divinely recycled.

O.D.

Overly dramatic. Ostracized damsel. Even orangutan descendent.

I knew it was too much when I pulled back on the needle and saw the luminescent liquid enter its insides. I had pondered other methods: cutting the wrists, a leap from a tenement roof. I knew this would hurl me out of the world in the worst of ways, but I didn't care. I was done. There was no thought of what it would feel like or what would happen if it didn't work. It was an spontaneous, instantaneous decision. I knew it had to be done. I injected the poison into myself and waited for it to course through my veins and shut down my organs one by one, liver, pancreas, lungs, and then my heart, my beating heart like a massive bloody drum sheltered within my ribcage pumping life through my body. It would slow down little by little and finally be still. The drum would go silent as death. I waited for death to find me.

I don't remember it, the first time I thought of suicide. I remember hearing about the kid who hung himself in the newspaper, and the girl who slit her wrists or took some pills. I've heard all the statistics. I must have been young, not even 14 yet. I'm an old soul, that's what my mother used to say. I tried like Jeffrey Eugenides to understand the emptiness of a creature who would put a razor to her veins and open her wrists, but I lived inside that creature. I lived in a dark in a world of people in the light. It was maddening. A mortal fleshy smelly imperfect inescapable prison. (I yearn for freedom.)

The first time I O.D'd though, it was a mistake. The human body gets used to substances over time, and gradually it requires more and more of the same substance to achieve a similar effect to the first attempt. I just pushed too much.

The world began to shake and spin, something like a roller coaster gone terribly wrong. I closed my eyes waiting for it pass. One minute, two, could have been hours. It's all relative or so said Einstein. Then liquid fire shot through my veins and I began to shake. I closed my eyes and waited for it to be over. There was nothing else I could do. I had made my metaphorical bed of with my actual one being this damp smelly alley. Then it was quiet. I was gone or at least I thought it was until I woke up in the hospital with a tube down my throat.

I woke up disoriented and confused,

I'd only been to the ER once before, for an ear infection when I was about 7. I was inconsolable and my parents panicked. Why are those the memories I keep?

THERE'S NO PLACE LIKE HOME AKA NOSTALGIA

I prepared myself for the journey back home. I had spent so long trying to forget that place ever existed, that I had a past and a history and a surname.

It's a strange feeling when the place you grew up no longer feels like home. The familiar streets, every sidewalk holding a memory, every building seeming like it has stood there for millennia. I begin to wonder where I belong. I feel as though I have no home. I'm an orphan.

(Driving through small towns, she loved to look left or right down the long roads that led away from the main street. I see a Mexican guy walking next to the train that seems to breathe life to this little town, dressed in a wife beater and loose jeans. I see him only for a split second but that is enough time for him to enter my imagination. Then I can make up his life, his history, his future. Where is he going? Where has he been? I like driving, seeing life as it happens, seeing it as it flashes by.)

As long as I didn't think about the past, I could pretend that it didn't happen. All I carried were memories of my inadequacy garnered over 2 decades. I never much felt close to my family except my parents who were the only people I confided in. It's difficult for me to relate to people. I worry that I'm not capable of empathy or love. I lived in my bedroom, feeling like too much of a social failure to be anywhere else. I looked in the mirror and inside at myself and saw everything that I wished I could change. Everything that made me undesirable. I felt ugly and stupid and useless. I was afraid I looked or smelled dirty which my parents said I did. I was afraid I wasn't saying the right thing. I was afraid I would get fat and remain even more alone if that was possible. I was full of fear and sadness and shame. I wallowed in them. I lived them day-in and day-out.

I have forgotten a lot of my life, a lot that happened to me, and not just because of the drugs. Even before that, I began losing huge chunks of my past. I think it happened subconsciously but purposefully. My mind was trying to protect me, by first rubbing the edges of a memory, the time and place and then the characters that appeared before the entire event became one that happened to someone else if I remembered it at all. Even memories that I wanted to keep close to me soon faded away like wisps of smoke. But everything was tinged with gray anyway so I didn't mind so much forgetting. I'd rather forget. Forgetting kept me sane. Who would we be if we remembered?

HITCHHIKING

I stood on the roadside under a cruel sun, thumb out waiting for someone to stop. Most cars just went speeding by without a glance. Only men would stop and more often than not, they wanted something in return. When I was younger, I dreamed of hitting the open road and letting fate take me where it may. But I never dreamed it would be like this. I had, after days, weeks mulling it over, decided to finally go back to where it began. I was going back home to face the life I had thrown away. In the program, they talked about how important it was to make amends with those we've hurt to move on and leave the past behind us. I had not bothered to do that until now. Only now had I seen that the past had chained me down where I stood and I wasn't moving forward. I couldn't. I had to break the chains of damage and hurt that bound me.

A Chevy pickup pulls over slowly. I walk over and bend down to look at the driver. He's in his mid-30s, plaid shirt, blue jeans, worn baseball cap, and he's wearing a smile that I know is trouble. But I'll take what life deals me. I get in.

"Where you from?"

"Nowhere."

"So what are you doing out here in the middle of nowhere?"

"Getting lost."

"You want to be found?" He put his hand on my thigh and grinned. His teeth were yellowed and his breath stank.

"Yeah, for fifty bucks."

"I don't pay for it, darling."

"I don't do charity work, honey."

"How about 30?"

"This isn't a negotiation. It's fifty or you'll have to do the heavy lifting yourself."

"Fine, but you better be worth it."

I imagined the whole scene like it was something that had already happened to me. But things were different. Or I wanted them to be different. Either way, I wasn't the person I used to be.

"You want to be found?"

I pushed his hand away. "I'll pass."

He struck my head hard with his fist. "I wasn't fucking asking, bitch."

I could taste the blood in my mouth. Another blow to the head, and I fell over. He was on top of me.

He kicked me out when he was finished. His odor clung on me like the smoke in a shithole bar. I stumbled to an overpass and sat down on the slanted cement face beneath it. I sat there for an eternity, waiting. For an epiphany? For a flood? For God?

Rain. I remember rain. Or maybe that is some theatrical invention of my damaged psyche. I couldn't tell you if it was dawn or twilight. Insanity has the distinct ability to blur details and indeed everything else until all you see is pain, a deluge of anguish that fills the empty abyss within you. My heart beats with a self-consuming sorrow, and I'm trapped in a nightmare from which I cannot wake. Every successive day is worse than the one that came before, and life is so long. Too long. I fear I have many, many days ahead of me. Suffering is not a tradition, it's a way of life. Struggle is habitual, and freedom is fantasy.

I sat there just staring at nothing, rocking back and forth, soaked to the bone wondering how I got here. Wondering how in the midst of trying to find joy I wound up here. I wonder about days past. About who I was and who I am. And who I am yet to be. The decisions I've made that haunt me or make me smile. Strange illuminated clouds curl above in the August afternoon sky, and I, the summation of all my experiences, search for words that have escaped, that have disappeared in the dark alleys and closed windows of my troubled mind. I wonder how much different my life would be had I chosen a different path. Would I be happier? In agony? Filled with regret? Where would life have taken me had I chosen a path?

I am filled with trepidation when I think of the days to come just as I would forget the days gone by if I could. Only the present is uncertain, with each moment becoming past and a new one taking its place. The harsh cycle of time, death, and renewal. Everyone has their place in the world, I suppose. But contentment is a different story altogether. The horizon stretches on forever, and a small universe lies between here and that place, that infinite mysterious place where dreams may come true.

STARRY DYNAMO

When I was a little girl, I remember wishing on stars. The house we lived in had a view of the stars from my bedroom, and I would look up between the blinds from my bed and hope that some unseen benevolent force was listening. I would close my eyes and ask earnestly with tears in my eyes that time could be turned back and I would never have been born. I believed if I wished hard enough, things would change. I would disappear and be saved both hell and the pain of life. I felt cheated in life, like in the poker game of existence, I had been dealt a shitty hand. No making lemonade from rotten lemons. Sorry for the shitty euphemism. When I got older, I realized the universe in its infinity complexity wasn't going to break every Einsteinian law of physics and relativity and send me back in time to be unborn, so instead I searched for more plausible options. Like death. An unlikely conclusion for an adolescent to reach but I was at the end of my rope, and it was beginning to fray.

ESCAPISM

She had built a universe around herself, with stars gliding brilliant as Apollo through the black infinity of the cosmos. Stars so hot that I would melt like ice if I dared venture too near. Stellar angels falling into black holes to be unmade. This was where I lived. In a such a quiet place

It was all ultimately about escapism. We watch movies, we do drugs, we live a different life in our heads. A place of euphoria and forgetfulness and dreams and laughter and love before we made the brisk and icy transition back to reality which feels like falling from a great height culminating in a collision with earth.

BATTLE SCARS

Rich scars on once smooth innocent adolescent skin. The twisted remnants of old battle scars, a constant reminder of the pain that lies behind, and a beckoning of the scars that are sure to come. It's difficult to live inside yourself, to have bored out a utopian universe in the dark recesses of your soul. I live there when I can for some small measure of happiness. But inevitably, I have to come back to reality, and all other worlds floating around inside my head recede into darkness. I'm left alone with my insanity, my troubled thoughts. My depression and despair. My suicide.

Time, measured out by scars, passed slowly with blood and torn flesh. Each scar represented a thousand tears.

I bore so many scars, many of them I had no memory of. So many nights I woke up and had no memory of the night before, but with bruises and in places that under normal circumstances should never see the light of the day. The next morning was the worst. Because my drug haze had faded and I woke up lucid, knowing exactly what I was doing to myself. I woke up ashamed, and it wasn't the pull of flight that called me back each time, but rather the desire to forget. I longed to forget. It was this desire that pulled me to dark alleys and dangerous neighborhoods after the sun sets. This desire that made me search out release, bargaining my body and soul for a devil's trade. My own brand of chemical comfort.

Sometimes I look back at the path my life has taken but I remind myself that I can't change the past as much as I want to. It's fixed forever, like a bad movie stuck on replay.

I'd always been the shy girl, the one who waited for other people to talk to her. That way I was sure they wanted to talk to her. As it was, many people didn't. I was an only child, so she didn't mind being alone. It was only when I had to be around others that she became uncomfortable. Only with people around was I lonely. I wanted to let others in but my awkwardness and insecurity prevented it. It seems like such a small thing but look at the lengths isolation can drive us to. Like all those who cannot fulfill their dreams, who cannot create, I wanted to destroy. I never before thought of myself of self-destructive, but I guess that's what I am. I imagine a ticking timer inside me just waiting to go off. I imagine spontaneously combusting as if I'd swallowed a stick of dynamite and the fuse was burning away. Then I imagined falling from the roof of one of the buildings I pass daily and shattering like glass into a millions pieces. Perhaps there is more beauty in destruction than creation. Perhaps the act of ripping down, of tearing, of unmaking is more human, more universally understood by those who are empty and trying to fill themselves with anything and everything. I imagined myself as I should have been.

HOME IS WHERE THE HEART IS

So there I was standing outside my parent's house. I hadn't been home in years. They probably thought I had died in some street somewhere, more nameless flotsam washed ashore amidst the drug current of America. I knew that once I knocked on the door, there was no going back. It was like crossing my metaphorical Rubicon, a distant shore on which I would be stranded.

My father will embrace me, my mother will cry. They'll tell me that the past is gone and that we can look toward the future as a family. We can start over and dear God, that's exactly what I need. A fresh start. A new life. Things start looking brighter like dawn in New York. The city's coming to life and the noises begin, a slow and building din that soon drowns out the world, swallows all the sound until silence is a distant memory. Sure the alleys still stink of piss and garbage but it's brighter, it's hopeful. It's a renewal of life to bring back all those lost in the dark.

But that never happened. I died somewhere between lost and found. More lost than found. More gone than here. I don't know if it was fate or chance, but it's fixed forever in the history of the world. And in my own personal history: the much too short years of my life.

Maybe the world is meant to be ironic. Or maybe we're meant to be in pain. No one gets just what they want. Those with their "whole lives ahead of them" die young, but those who have no desire to live either suffer daily for most of a century or resort to the pill, the pistol, or the false perceptions and perish. I have lived my years, few as they may seem, and I am old and weary of the world.

WHAT BEGINS MUST ALSO END

Well, that's it. That's my story. It's not sugar coated, nothing Norman Rockwell would ever dream of painting. But it's mine. I wish I had all the answers. I wish I could tell you something transcendent that shakes you to your soul. I think more than anything I wanted to be one of those poor souls who has some divine rapture. Who is rescued by an omniscient deity who won't let us fall into ruin. Maybe I should steal the words of another great writer but that hardly seems right. All I can say is I lived and I died. At least we are all made equal in death. But whatever the story, it must come to an end. And at least now I am free.

Appendix 1

Winter

The tea in her hands was a refuge, a sanctuary from the grey morning. She had her ritual, blowing into the mug so the stream drifted across her face like a warm front moving across water. She closed her eyes and nearly fell asleep where she sat. It was a long restless night full of haunting dreams that would not let her rest. Dark figures moving in the streets below, cries from suspicious alleys. Gene was up before her, dressed and gone when she heaved her body out of bed. She balanced there for a moment on the edge of the bed, looking down as if over a great precipice or the ledge outside their apt window. Then she rose and made her way slowly to the bathroom.

This was his apartment and she'd only been in it for 6 months. Gene was a photographer, a rather successful one, 17 years her senior and with a 14 year old son of his own he shared with his ex, a woman who had once been beautiful but now showed her age, much like he did. She felt like a tenant here--or better--a guest. She didn't touch or move anything, respecting the sanctity of this museum that he deigned to share. They had met a year and a half before at one of his gallery showings. He was a bit awkward and talked with his hands and his idiosyncrasies matched her own. He had a childish joy in the world that amused her but she wasn't so sure if what drifted between them was love or just companionship. She was grateful he had never judged her scars, the ones lining her arms and leg and the telltale remnants of an attempt at ripping herself body from soul. He only asked questions and patiently listened. But now they had their routines, their measured procedures at filling up the day. Even sex had become rote and predictable. Him on top and her trying desperately to grasp at any past memory to wake her passion. She had begun to fake it. She thought of this now as she ate her scrambled eggs and homemade smoothie. Then she grabbed her laptop and made her way down to a local coffeeshop of which there seemed to be an infinite amount in NYC. She went there to write and for a change of scenery, and on rare days, some inspiration.

She was a writer: a novelist and poet. For many years, it seemed an impossibility after so many failed attempts at being published. She had settled for crushed dreams and began doing mindless work in front of a computer screen 8 hours a day in a cubicle in a sea of cubicles, each one more hopeless than the next. Deciding that she could not bear this fate, she made one last ditch effort, sending her work off to dozens of publishers and receiving back as many rejection letters like dead fish on the end of a line. It was over. It was all over. The fat lady, whoever the hell she was, had sung a final sad melody and she went into the bathroom and opened her flesh with a razor. It was a long time coming however, her depression having been a constant since jr. high. She was never treated or medicated for it. Self-diagnosed. It had come to define her. Part of her character, her personality, a defining trait like her dark eyes or dark curls and she let it. Let it rule her, having not the strength or desire to combat this lurking thing. She felt it in the bathtub with her that day, a bloody compatriot witness to it all. But somehow, she had survived.

She scooped up her laptop and purse and walked the 12 blocks back to the apt. Gene had a show at a gallery near Times Square. She had to get ready, choosing a red dress and black heels. Flat-twisting her hair in rows going back to the nape of her neck and securing them in a ponytail. She stood by the living room window watching the urbanites scurry about through a cavernous steel jungle. Like a powerless god, she watches these unknowable beings live out their lives. Gene comes through the door, frantic, nervous, kisses her.

"Heyhonyoulookgorgeous," and moves into the bedroom to ready himself. He come out ina black shirt and black slacks. Simplicity. Kisses her again.

"Ready?"

She nods, gives a half-hearted smile. She hates these things, hates the crowds, the uncomfortable formal wear that never quite looks right on her, the food, the pretention. She goes for Gene because she wants to seem supportive. At the Titrich Gallery, his photos are blown up to King Kong proportion, like Guernica in Madrid, occupying their own walls, their own universes. His art is haunting, at times bizarre. A couple disturb her. She drifts away from him like she always does at these thing, moving through the room unhurried, glancing at each piece until she arrives at hers. Hers in the sense that it is her massive face which occupies the space--well, just the eyes. She was lying on her stomach in bed after she and Glen had made love one morning and he had jumped up, fully naked, to capture her image, to steal her essence. Her face hidden by her hair like a goddess in repose. It was months ago back when she was still trying to hold to spontaneity and the first flush, the earliest amorous feelings she had for this man before the malaise set in.

Now she wandered through the gallery like a nomad, selecting others at random and wondering if they were happy or fulfilled or just miserable but unable to remove their comedic masks.

In front of a photo of a procession of Spaniards wearing medieval penitent hoods for Semana Santa (which resemble the garb of the Ku Klux Klan), she paused to study it. A man approached wearing a suit and tie.

"Do you like it?" His accent wasn't American.

"I like the way the artist plays with light and darkness."

"And are you a connoisseur of art or an occasional admirer?"

"What's the difference?"

"The willingness to spend obscene amounts of money."

"Which one are you?"

"I just love art. It gives us the power to define our own humanity."

"Wow, did you come up with that line all by yourself?"

He laughed. "Yeah, I did."

"So where are you from, Mr….?"

"Just Noah. I'm from Johannesburg."

"Why so far afield?"

"Business."

"That's very vague."

"I'm trying to remain mysterious."

"Okay, Mr. Noah No-Last-Name from Johannesburg, which piece do you like?"

"The one of you."

"You recognize me?"

"How could I not recognize such a beautiful woman?"

She is flattered but also thinking he's full of shit. She laughs and looks down and back up, playing the bashful dame. Just then as if sense she was flirting, Gene appears, all dark hair and blue eyes, hair graying at his chin, he puts an arm around her waist, laying claim, and looks at Noah.

"Hi, hon," he says and kisses her cheek.

"Um, Gene, this is Noah, Noah, Gene."

"Great to meet you. I love your work."

"Thanks, it's great to have my work appreciated."

It was written on Noah's face. Damn, she has a boyfriend.

"Come on, babe. I have some people I want you to meet."

I extend my hand. "Nice to have met you, Noah." I just wanted to touch him, to be touched.

That night, Gene and I make love like we haven't in a long time. But I know this is only because Noah is still on my mind. I imagined his hand caressing my breasts, his lips on my neck, I imagine him inside me. No faking this time.

Life took up its usual course, a river through a well-run canyon. I was nearly finished with my novel and had started going on walks in the park. Gene was on to his next series of photos with some existential title I can't remember. I had carved out a niche of indifference and was quite comfortable in it until I realized that my growing nausea and the fact my elusive period had not visited me in some months was a herald of arrival. My God, I'm pregnant. The whole world fell out of focus. The nausea rose up and lifted its cruel head, a rough beast slouching toward Bethelehem. I vomited. Then I cried. At first I didn't know why--the floodgates would not close--but soon I realized it was because I pitied this poor sad little thing growing inside me. This thing cursed with me as a mother, doomed to be born in a house without love. Did Gene even want another child? We had never even spoken of it. I couldn't imagine him wanting to start over at his age and with a son closer to college than the cradle. I went to the mantel and the side table in the living room and saw pictures of Gene with his son when he was just a boy being carried on his shoulders or holding his hand at some family outing. His son loved him. Even now as a teenager, he still worshipped him.

As for me, I never wanted kids. Somewhere deep inside I knew they'd be as screwed up as I am. I always thought the gift I'd give my unborn children would be that of never having been born. Should I tell

Gene? Await his reaction? Or should I just silently end it and keep that secret for the rest of my life?

Gene came home from the studio. She was waiting for him on the couch. She moved with purpose, grabbing his hand and leading him back to the sofa where she sat him down and took a seat next to him.

She held his face in her hands and searched his eyes. She knew what she was looking for, the man that she had loved once long ago. She searched for the man that had made her laugh, that had loved her with those eyes, that had held her in his arms through star-strewn nights, whose nervousness had endeared him to her. She desperately sought hope in his eyes, hope that she could fall in love with him again, that they could be a family, that he could fix whatever damage was hidden away inside her and make her a good mother but she saw nothing. Only the wisps of something that was once there but something that had long since fled and left ruin in its wake. She wept.

Gene held her softly to his chest, his brow furrowed.

In this moment, her life split like a river into infinite streams. It branched out across time each flowing its own way at its own pace and each spilling into endless seas that exist without names or boundaries. It was in this moment that her fate would be decided, that she would choose one stream to sail and never return to her tributary, to this place. Perhaps she tells him the truth and is resurrected from her melancholy, and her maternal instincts, gifts from 1,000 generations of mothers, will awaken. She will appear in photos on the mantelpiece holding an infant. Or perhaps she says nothing and lets the silence unmake her like a black hole erasing what little lied between them.

"I'm pregnant," she says quietly. Her course is set. All that remains is the map that will lead her, the sails that will carry her, and the child that will follow.

www.ingramcontent.com/pod-product-compliance
Ingram Content Group UK Ltd.
Pitfield, Milton Keynes, MK11 3LW, UK
UKHW041834200726
13854UKWH00003BA/1134